"Peekaboo. I see you," I said.

Then I laughed and laughed. 'Cause I'm a laugh a minute, that's why.

I kept on laughing at that funny joke.

Only too bad for me.

'Cause after a while, I couldn't even stop.

I was out of control, I think.

I holded my sides and fell on the ground.

Then I rolled and laughed and rolled and laughed. All around in the grass.

Handsome Warren looked nervous of me.

He backed up.

"What a nutball," he said very soft.

The Junie B. Jones series by Barbara Park

Junie B. Jones
Loves
Handsome Warren

by Barbara Park
illustrated by Denise Brunkus

SCHOLASTIC INC.
New York Toronto London Auckland Sydney
Mexico City New Delhi Hong Kong

ISBN 0-439-13074-3

12 11 10 9 8 7 6   2 3 4/0

Printed in the U.S.A.   40

First Scholastic printing, November 1999

Contents

1/ Handsome Warren

My name is Junie B. Jones. The B stands for Beatrice. Except I don't like Beatrice.

I just like B and that's all.

I am in the grade of kindergarten.

My room is named Room Nine.

I have two bestest friends at that place.

One of them is named Lucille.

She is way beautifuller than me. That's because her nanna buys her fancy dresses. Plus also she has lacy socks with ribbons on them.

My other friend is named Grace. Me

and that Grace ride the school bus together.

She has my favorite kind of hair. It is called *automatically curly*.

Also, she has pink high tops. And fast feet.

That Grace is the fastest runner in all of kindergarten.

She wins me at all of our races.

I am a good sport about it. Except for sometimes I call her the name of *cheater pants*.

Me and that Grace and Lucille play horses together before school.

Horses is when you gallop. And trot. And snort.

I am Brownie. Lucille is Blackie. And that Grace is Yellowie.

Only today, me and that Grace couldn't find Lucille anywhere.

We looked all over the place for her.

"Darn it," I said. "Now we can't play horses that good. 'Cause two horses isn't as fun as three horses."

"Maybe she's just late," said that Grace. "Or else maybe something went wrong at her house."

I tapped on my chin very thinking.

"Yes," I said. "Maybe her grampa brought a parrot to her house. And Lucille was getting dressed for school. And then the parrot flew into her room. And he got all tangled up in her hair. And so her grampa had to call 911. And a real live fireman came to her house. And he cut the parrot out of her hair with scissors. Only that left a teeny baldy spot. But guess what? If you wear a big bow, nobody can even tell the difference."

That Grace looked curious at my big bow.

I did a gulp.

"Yeah, only pretend I didn't even tell you that," I said very soft.

After that, me and that Grace looked for Lucille some more.

And guess what?

I spotted her! That's what!

"HEY, GRACE! I SEE HER! I SEE LUCILLE! SHE IS RUNNING PAST THE WATER FOUNTAIN!"

That Grace spotted her, too.

"HEY! SOMEBODY'S CHASING HER, JUNIE B.!" she yelled. "WHO *IS* THAT BOY? WHO IS THAT BOY WHO IS CHASING LUCILLE?"

I squinted my eyes very harder.

"IT IS AN EVIL *STRANGER BOY*,

GRACE!" I shouted back. "AN EVIL STRANGER BOY IS CHASING LUCILLE! AND SO NOW YOU AND ME WILL HAVE TO SAVE HER!"

I waved my arm in a fast circle.

"Come on, Yellowie! Let's go! Let's go save Lucille!"

Then me and that Grace springed into action!

We galloped our fastest after the stranger!

That Grace caught up to him speedy quick.

She shooed her arms all around.

"GO AWAY, BOY! GO AWAY AND LEAVE LUCILLE ALONE!" she shouted.

"YES!" I yelled. "LEAVE LUCILLE ALONE! OR I WILL TELL PRINCIPAL ON YOU! 'CAUSE ME AND HIM ARE PERSONAL FRIENDS. AND HE

WILL POUND YOUR HEAD!"

After that, me and that Grace kept on shooing our arms until he ran away.

Then we did a high five.

"HURRAY!" we shouted. "HURRAY! HURRAY! WE SAVED LUCILLE FROM THE EVIL STRANGER BOY!"

All of a sudden, Lucille came stomping at us very angry.

"WHY DID YOU DO THAT?" she hollered. "WHY DID YOU CHASE THAT BOY AWAY? NOW YOU'VE RUINED *EVERYTHING*!"

Me and that Grace looked surprised at her.

"But we thought you *wanted* us to do that," said that Grace.

"We saved you from the evil stranger

boy," I explained very proud.

Lucille did a mad breath.

"He is *not* an evil stranger boy, Junie B.! He's a new kid in Room Eight. And his name is Warren! And he's the handsomest boy I ever saw! He's even been in a *TV* commercial before!"

Me and that Grace raised up our eyebrows.

"He has?" said that Grace.

"He's been in a TV commercial before?" I said.

That Grace stood on her tippy-toes.

"Where did he go? I didn't even get a good look at him," she said.

"Me too," I said. "I didn't get a good look at him, too. How handsome is he, Lucille? Is he handsome like a movie star?"

Just then, that Grace jumped up and down very excited.

"THERE HE IS! THERE HE IS! HE'S OVER THERE UNDER THAT TREE! SEE HIM, JUNIE B.? SEE HIM?"

I squinted my hardest at that guy.

Then my eyes practically popped out of my head!

'Cause he *was* handsome like a movie star! That's why!

"Wowie-wow-wow! What a *chunk*!" I said. "I would like him for my new boyfriend, I think!"

Lucille made angry eyes at me.

"No!" she hollered. "Don't say that, Junie B.! He can't be *your* boyfriend. He can only be *my* boyfriend. 'Cause I saw him first!"

I thought it over very careful.

"Yeah, only here's the problem, Lucille," I said. "Me and Grace didn't actually get a crack at him yet."

"Yeah," said that Grace. "We definitely need a crack at him. And so now you have to introduce us."

Lucille stamped her foot.

"No!" she yelled. "No! No! No! 'Cause you guys will steal him away from me! And that's not even fair! Plus, Junie B. already *has* a boyfriend. Remember, Junie B.? You already have Ricardo! Remember?"

I did another peek at Handsome Warren.

"Yeah, only I think I may be ready to move on," I said very quiet.

That's when Lucille's face got boiling mad. And she stomped away from us speedy quick.

Only me and that Grace didn't even care.

We just kept peeking and peeking at that handsome boy.

'Cause he was beauty to our eyes.

2/ Pigs

Lucille sits next to me in Room Nine.

I kept on being nice to her.

'Cause I wanted to meet that handsome boy, of course.

"Want to be friends again, Lucille? Huh? Want to be friends like we used to be? That would be nice of us, don't you think?"

"No," said Lucille. "You only want to be friends so you can steal my new boyfriend."

I did a big breath at her.

"Yeah, only how can I even steal him,

Lucille?" I asked. "'Cause you are way beautifuller than me. Remember that? Remember how beautifuller than me you are?"

Lucille remembered.

She fluffed herself.

Then she showed me her new lacy socks.

"Eight dollars and fifty cents...*not* including tax," she said.

I bugged out my eyes at them.

"Wowie-wow-wow. Those are some fancy feet you have there, madam!" I said.

After that, I showed Lucille *my* socks, too.

"See, Lucille? See mine? They are very sagging and droopy. That's because last night me and my dog Tickle played tug-of-war with those things. And he got drooly on them."

Lucille made a face.

"Eew," she said.

"I know they are eew," I said back. "That's what I've been trying to tell you, Lucille. I am a big pig. And so how can I even steal your boyfriend?"

Just then, Lucille looked nicer at me.

I scooted my chair close to her.

"Now we are friends again! Right, Lucille? Right?" I said. "And so now you can introduce me to Handsome Warren. 'Cause I won't even steal that guy."

Lucille fluffed herself some more.

"I don't know…I'll think about it," she said.

I clapped my hands real thrilled.

Then I quick stood up on my chair.

"GRACE! HEY, GRACE!" I hollered. "LUCILLE SAID SHE'LL THINK ABOUT IT!"

Just then, I heard a different voice.

"JUNIE B. JONES! WHAT DO YOU THINK YOU ARE DOING?"

It was my teacher.

Her name is Mrs.

She has another name, too. But I just like Mrs. and that's all.

I smiled kind of nervous.

"I am trying to get a message to Grace,"
I said very soft.

Mrs. hurried up to my table.

"Never *ever* stand up in your chair, Junie

B.," she said. "You could fall off and break something."

"Yeah!" shouted a meanie boy named Jim. "She could break the *floor* with her hard *head*!"

I made a fist at that kid.

"PLUS ALSO I COULD BREAK YOUR WHOLE ENTIRE BEAN BRAIN!" I hollered back.

Mrs. plopped me back in my seat.

"That's enough," she grouched. "I mean it, Junie B. Not one more word."

After that, I stayed in my chair very good. And I did my work.

I did my spelling.

And my arithmetic.

And my printing.

Also, I drew a sausage patty on my arm.

Only that wasn't even an assignment.

That is called *working on your own*.

Pretty soon, Mrs. clapped her loud hands together.

"Okay, everyone. It's almost time for recess. Pass in your papers and line up at the door."

Mrs. looked at me.

"And please...let's be ladies and gentlemen about it."

Ladies and gentlemen means No Trampling Thy Neighbor.

It is a Ten Commandments, I think.

Me and Lucille held hands.

"Now you're gonna introduce me. Right, Lucille? Now I'm gonna get to meet that handsome boy."

Just then, that Grace runned up behind us.

I was happy to see her.

"Grace! Grace! Guess what? Lucille is going to introduce us to Handsome Warren! 'Cause you and me are big pigs, that's why!"

That Grace looked upset at me.

"I am *not* a big pig," she said.

I quick whispered in her ear. "Yeah, only

19

we're not *really* big pigs, Grace. We just have to *say* we're big pigs. Or else Lucille thinks we will steal her boyfriend. Get it?"

That Grace got it.

"I am a giant stink hog," she said to Lucille.

And so after that, all of us skipped to the swing set very happy.

We sat down. And waited for Room Eight to come out.

We waited a real long time.

Then all of a sudden, Room Eight opened their door! And Handsome Warren came out of there!

Lucille runned to him and grabbed his hand.

She pulled him to the swings to meet us.

"*That* is Grace. And *that* is Junie B. Jones," she said to Handsome Warren.

He waved very cute and friendly.

I quick hided behind my hands.

'Cause all of a sudden I felt shy of that guy.

I peeked through my fingers.

"Peekaboo. I see you," I said.

Then I laughed and laughed. 'Cause I'm a laugh a minute, that's why.

I kept on laughing at that funny joke.

Only too bad for me.

'Cause after while, I couldn't even stop.

I was out of control, I think.

I holded my sides and fell on the ground.

Then I rolled and laughed and rolled and laughed. All around in the grass.

Handsome Warren looked nervous of me.

He backed up.

"What a nutball," he said very soft.

Then he turned around. And walked away.

And Lucille and that Grace walked with him.

3/ Not a Nutball

Mrs. blew her whistle.

That means *come in from recess*.

Lucille and that Grace ran to get me.

'Cause I was still in the grass, that's why.

Lucille was happy and sparkly.

"Didn't you *love* him, Junie B.? Wasn't he so handsome? He was even handsomer up close, don't you think? He was nice, too. Wasn't he nice?"

That Grace was happy and sparkly, too.

"He said he liked my high tops," she told me.

"He said he liked my dress," said Lucille.

"He said I was a nutball," I said.

Lucille twirled all around.

"Not me," she said. "He didn't say *I* was a nutball. That's because he loves me!"

That Grace jumped high in the air.

"Me too! He loves me, too!" she said real squealy.

Just then, Lucille stopped twirling.

She crossed her arms.

"No, Grace," she said. "He does *not* love you, too. He only loves me. 'Cause I saw him first. And you're not allowed to steal him away, remember?"

That Grace crossed *her* arms, too.

"I'm not *stealing* him away, Lucille. He just automatically loves me on his own. And there's nothing I can do about it," she said.

I tugged on Lucille's dress.

"How come he said I was a nutball, do you think? Why did he have to say that dumb thing?"

Lucille didn't pay attention to me. She kept on being mad at that Grace.

"I knew it!" she grouched. "I knew this was going to happen, Grace! You're trying to steal my boyfriend! Junie B. said you wouldn't! But you are!"

She looked down at me.

"Tell her, Junie B.! Tell Grace she can't steal my boyfriend!"

I looked curious at her.

"I am not a nutball. Am I? Am I a nutball?" I said. "I am not a nutball."

Just then, that Grace leaned close to Lucille's nose.

"I CAN LOVE ANYBODY I WANT
TO, LUCILLE!" she hollered in her face.
"NO, YOU CANNOT, GRACE!"
"YES, I CAN, *TOO*, LUCILLE!"

I tapped on both their ankles.

"How many think I'm a nutball? Raise your hand," I said.

Just then, Mrs. blew her whistle again.

And so I stood up from the grass. And I walked to Room Nine all by myself.

'Cause I couldn't stop thinking about being a nutball, that's why.

I thought about it the whole rest of the day.

I didn't even talk.

Not at Show-and-Tell.

Not at snacktime.

Not even when I got on the bus to ride home.

That Grace sat down next to me. She was happy and sparkly again.

"I *know* he loves me better than Lucille," she said. "I'm positive he does. And he hasn't even seen how fast I can run yet."

She poked me with her finger.

"Who do you think he likes better? Me or Lucille? And tell the truth," she said.

I still didn't talk.

That Grace jiggled me.

"How come you're not talking, Junie B.?" she asked. "How come you're not answering me? Are you sick? Do you have a sore throat?"

Just then, her eyes opened real wide. And her whole mouth came open.

"Ohhhhh...I know why you're not talking. It's because you're upset, right? You're upset that you're a nutball."

I spinned around at her very quick.

"I am *not* a nutball, Grace! I am just a regular normal girl. And I don't even know why that boy had to call me that!"

"*I* do," said that Grace. "I know why he called you that. It's because you couldn't stop laughing. And you fell in the grass. And you rolled all around down there."

I stared at her.

"Yeah? So?" I said.

"So that's how nutballs act," said that Grace. "And I should know. 'Cause I have a nutball right in my own personal family."

I raised up my eyebrows.

"You do?" I said.

"Yes," she said. "My two-year-old brother Jeffie is a nutball. Every time we go to the mall, we have to put him on a leash. Or else he tackles people. And then he hides in the clothes and Security has to come."

She looked at me very suspicious.

"Did *you* ever do that, Junie B. Jones? Hmmm? Did *you* ever tackle people? And hide in the clothes and Security had to come?"

I quick looked away from her.

'Cause that is my own personal beeswax.

"Jeffie's not allowed to eat sugar cereal anymore, either," said that Grace. "My mother thinks the sugar gets him all jazzied up."

She raised one eyebrow very curious.

"Do *you* eat sugar cereal for breakfast, Junie B.? Hmmm? *Do* you?" she asked.

I looked away again.

'Cause guess what?

More of my own personal beeswax. That's what.

4/ Fibers

It was the next morning.

I gave Tickle my sugar cereal.

I gave him my Sweetie Puffs. And my Crackle Berries. And my Happy Smacky Flakes.

He loved eating that stuff very much.

Then he runned in the living room. And he throwed up on the rug.

Mother screamed real loud.

That's how come I hided under the sink. But she and Daddy found me there.

They did not handle theirselves that
professional.

"WHY, JUNIE B.? WHY WOULD YOU
DO SUCH A THING!" shouted Daddy
very loud.

"DO WE HAVE TO WATCH YOU EVERY MINUTE?" shouted Mother very loud.

Just then, my grandma Helen Miller walked in the front door.

"Grandma Miller! Grandma Miller! I love you! I love you!" I shouted.

Then I runned to her speedy fast. And I hided in her coat till Mother and Daddy left for work.

After that, my grandma let me pick a new cereal to eat.

I picked a grown-up kind.

It was the kind with fibers in it.

"This kind is good for me. Right, Grandma? This kind won't even jazzy me up."

Then I put that delicious stuff in my mouth.

And I chewed and chewed. Only it didn't actually grind up that good.

I chewed on it the whole entire morning.

I was still chewing when that Grace got on my school bus.

She ran to me very excited.

"Look, Junie B.! Look what my mother bought me!" she said.

She holded up her foot.

"New running shoes!" she said. "See them? See the lightning stripes on the sides! That means I can run as fast as lightning! And so now Warren will love me the best for sure!"

I pointed at my mouth.

"Yeah, only I can't actually discuss this right now, Grace. 'Cause I'm chewing fibers here," I said.

I opened up to show her.

"See them in there? They are stuck in my teeth, I think."

After that, I poked all around with my fingernail. And I sucked them out.

I smacked my lips together.

"Good news. I think I'm done," I said.

That Grace tried to show me her shoes again.

"Yeah, only sorry, Grace. But I still can't talk yet. 'Cause I have to do something very important."

Then I leaned back in my seat.

And I closed my eyes.

And I didn't move for lots of seconds.

All of a sudden, I clapped my hands very joyful.

"Did you *see* me, Grace? Did you see how *calm* I was just then? That's because I don't have sugar in me today! And I can sit still very excellent!"

I hugged her real tight.

"It worked, Grace! The fiber cereal worked! Now I'm not a nutball anymore! And so Handsome Warren will love me just like he loves you!"

That Grace did not look happy.

She bended down and dusted her new shoes.

I bended down there with her.

"How come you're not happy, Grace? How come you're not happy that he will love me, too?" I asked.

She did a huffy breath.

"You're breathing on the shoes," she said. "Don't breathe on the shoes."

Just then, the bus stopped at school.

I looked out the window and clapped my hands real thrilled.

"Grace! Grace! I see Handsome Warren! He's at the water fountain! And Lucille isn't even there yet!"

All of a sudden that Grace's face got very perky.

She zoomed off the bus like a speeding bullet. And she ran to Handsome Warren zippity quick.

I could hear her shouting all over the playground.

"LOOK, WARREN! LOOK AT MY NEW SHOES!" she yelled. "THEY HAVE LIGHTNING ON THE SIDES! SEE?"

She was running in circles around that handsome guy.

"Wanna have a race?" she asked him. "Wanna see how fast I am? Bet you can't beat me, Warren! Bet you can't beat me in a race!"

And so just then, Handsome Warren and that Grace raced all over the playground.

And he couldn't even beat her.

He came back very pooped.

"Wow," he said. "You're the fastest runner I ever saw. Maybe someday you'll be in the Olympics."

"I will, Warren!" said that Grace. "I will be in the Olympics someday! Wanna race me again? Huh? Do you?"

Just then, Lucille popped in out of nowhere.

She had on the beautifullest dress I ever saw.

She spinned all around.

"Ooooo, Lucille. You look like a royal highness in that thing," I said.

"I know it," she said. "This is the kind of dress that *princesses* wear. It is made out of rich red velvet."

She twirled in front of Handsome Warren.

"This dress costed over one hundred and

fifty dollars…*not* including tax," she said.

All of a sudden, Handsome Warren's eyes got big and wide.

"Wow! You must be the richest girl in the whole school!" he said.

Lucille fluffed her hair.

"I am," she said. "I *am* the richest girl in the whole school, Warren. Guess how much my shoes cost? Just guess, okay?"

Just then I jumped right in front of that guy's face.

"Hello. How are you today?" I said very pleasant. "I am fine. I am fine and calm."

He backed up from me.

"Yeah, only you don't even have to be afraid," I said. "'Cause I ate fibers for breakfast. And I am so calm I could go to sleep, probably. Want to see me? Huh, Warren? Want to see me go to sleep?"

I plopped down in the grass.

"Look, Warren. See me down here? I am
not even laughing and rolling. I am just
being calm. And that's all."

I put my head on the ground.

"Watch me go to sleep, Warren. Watch me. Watch me."

I closed my eyes and opened them again.

"Did you see that, Warren? Huh? Did you see me go to sleep? See? I *told* you I was calm. Didn't I? Huh? Didn't I tell you?"

Handsome Warren looked and looked at me.

Then he did the cuckoo sign.

And he walked away to the swings.

And Lucille and that Grace walked with him.

5/ Hurray for Princess Clothes!

That night at dinner, a great idea came in my head.

It came during my macaroni.

"HEY! I JUST THOUGHT OF IT!" I shouted. "I JUST THOUGHT OF HOW TO GET THAT HANDSOME GUY TO LOVE ME!"

I stuffed in more macaroni.

"HURRY, EVERYBODY! EAT! EAT!

WE GOTTA GET TO THE MALL BEFORE IT CLOSES!"

Just then, two macaronis fell out of my mouth. And onto the floor. And my dog named Tickle ate them.

Daddy made a face.

"Hey, hey, hey! Slow down! What's the hurry?" he said.

"We gotta get to the mall! That's what's the hurry! We have to buy me a princess dress! Plus also I need some shoes with lightning!"

Mother and Daddy looked funny at me.

That's how come I had to explain all about Handsome Warren. And how he loved Lucille's princess dress. And how he loved Grace's fast shoes.

"And so now *I* will get a princess dress! Plus also I will get shoes with lightning! And then Warren will love *me*, too!"

I wiped my mouth with my hand. Then I quick jumped down from my chair.

"'Scuse me, please! 'Scuse me from the table! 'Cause I'm all filled up!"

I runned down the hall. And zoomed into the nursery.

The nursery is where my baby brother named Ollie lives.

"YOU GUYS DO THE DISHES!" I hollered to Mother and Daddy. "I'LL PUT OLLIE'S SWEATER ON HIS HEAD! 'CAUSE THAT WILL SAVE US TIME, I THINK!"

I quick climbed into Ollie's crib.

Then I tried to pull that baby's sweater on him. Only his giant head didn't fit through the hole.

He waked up from his nap.

Then he started to cry very loud.

I heard loud feet running in the hall.

"JUNIE B. JONES! WHAT DO YOU THINK YOU ARE DOING?" yelled an angry voice.

It was Mother.

She runned in the room. And picked up baby Ollie.

She patted his giant head.

"That's quite a melon he has there," I said very quiet.

Baby Ollie kept on crying.

"Want me to get a leash?" I asked Mother. "Let's put him on a leash, okay? 'Cause he is all jazzied up, I think. And so how will we even control him at the mall?"

Mother rolled her eyes way back in her head.

"We're not *going* to the mall, Junie B.," she said. "We are not going anywhere."

I stamped my foot.

"Yes!" I said. "We *have* to! We *have* to go to the mall to get my princess dress! And my shoes with lightning. Or else that boy will not love me, I tell you!"

Mother closed her eyes. She did some deep breaths.

Her voice got softer.

"Okay. I want you to listen to me. And I want you to listen carefully," she said. "You don't make friends by wearing new dresses or shoes with lightning. You make new friends by being fun to be with. And by being nice to people. And by caring about their feelings."

She lifted me out of the crib.

"And *honesty* is important, too, Junie B.," she said. "You have to be *honest* with people. And that means that you can't pretend to be someone you're not."

She smoothed my hair.

"You're *not* Lucille, Junie B. And you're not Grace, either. You're just *you*. You're just Junie B. Jones. And believe me, that's a big enough job for *anyone*."

I did a sniffle. Also I did a snort and a swallow.

"Yeah, only I *know* I am Junie B. Jones," I said. "I just want to be Junie B. Jones in a *princess* dress."

I put my head on her shoulder.

"Didn't you ever want a princess dress when you were a little girl?" I asked. "Huh, Mother? Didn't you?"

Mother didn't answer. She was thinking it over probably.

Just then, I looked over her shoulder.

I saw a new toy on baby Ollie's shelf.

"Hey! What's that, Mother? What's that on that shelf there? Is that a new teddy bear I see?"

I runned and pulled that guy down.

"Look, Mother! Look what this bear is wearing! It is a ribbon made out of rich, red velvet! And that is 'zactly the kind of cloth I've been looking for!"

I took the bow off the teddy. And I held it next to my hair.

"How do I look? Huh, Mother? Do I

look like a beautiful princess? Do I look gorgeous? Huh? Do I?"

Just then, I felt happy and sparkly inside.

I quick kissed Mother and zoomed out of the room.

'Cause maybe there was more princess clothes right in my very own house!

6/ Speechless

The next day, that Grace saw me on the bus.

Her mouth came all the way open.

I smiled very gorgeous.

"I know why you're looking at me like that, Grace," I said. "Mother said when people saw me, they would be speechless."

I fluffed my hair.

"Speechless is when your mouth can't speech," I explained.

That Grace pointed at my neck.

"What is *that*? Is that a *dog* collar you're wearing?" she said.

I laughed and laughed at her.

"You sillyhead, Grace!" I said. "Don't you know anything? This is a lovely collar of jewels! It is the kind of jewels that princesses wear! Only I didn't even know we had this gorgeous thing! I found it where Mother keeps the dog food. Only I don't actually know why it got put there."

I holded out my arms.

"And did you notice *these*, Grace? Did you notice my long white princess gloves? They are the kind of gloves that Cinderella wears. And Cinderella is a real, actual princess. Plus also she does floors."

I pointed at my head.

"And what about this golden crown I am wearing? It is from a real actual Dairy

Queen! Plus, also I have red velvet bows on my sneakers! And Mother even drew lightning on their sides. Just like yours!"

I twirled all around.

"Just wait till Handsome Warren gets a load of me now! Right, Grace? Now that guy will have to love me! 'Cause who wouldn't?"

Grace slumped down in her seat.

She didn't talk the whole rest of the way to school.

And guess what else? When the bus got to school, she didn't even wait for me again.

She ran right straight to Handsome Warren without me.

I tried to race her. But my collar of jewels scratched my neck. Plus also my golden crown fell off my head.

Handsome Warren was sitting on the ground.

His face was hiding in his knees.

I pushed my way in front of Lucille and that Grace.

Then I tapped him on the head.

"Hello. How are you today? I am wearing princess clothes," I told him.

Handsome Warren didn't look up.

I tapped on his head again.

"Yeah, only I actually think you should get a load of me. 'Cause Grandma Miller says I am quite a sight," I said.

Lucille rolled her eyes.

"It won't do you any good to talk to him, Junie B.," she said. "He's not talking to anyone."

"Not even to *me*," said that Grace.

I squatted down next to that guy. And stared real hard.

"How come you're not talking? Huh, Warren? Does the cat have your tongue?"

I waited very patient.

Then I leaned closer to his ear.

"I SAID, DOES THE CAT HAVE YOUR TONGUE, WARREN?"

All of a sudden, Handsome Warren raised up his head.

"GO AWAY!" he shouted. "ALL OF YOU! GO AWAY AND LEAVE ME ALONE!"

I stayed squatted a real long time.

Then I stood up very quiet. And I looked at that Grace and Lucille.

"Good news," I said. "He talked."

After that, all of us kept on standing there and standing there.

'Cause we didn't actually know how to handle this situation, that's why.

Finally, Lucille did a huffy breath at him.

"You're not being nice, Warren. You

used to be nice. But now you're not. And so I don't even want to be your friend today."

"Me, either," said that Grace. "I don't want to be your friend today, either!"

Then both of those guys held hands. And they stomped away from there very furious.

Handsome Warren raised up one eyeball to see if they were gone.

I quick bended down and looked into it.

"Hello. How are you today?" I said. "I am wearing princess clothes."

Handsome Warren did a groan.

Then he closed his eyeball. And he hided his face again.

7 / Knock Knock

I sat down next to Handsome Warren.

"Guess what? I'm not even going to bother you," I said. "I'm just going to sit here. And mind my own personal beeswax. And that's all."

I thought a little bit.

"Plus here's another good thing. You don't even have to look at my princess clothes if you don't want to. 'Cause clothes is not how I make friends," I said.

Handsome Warren didn't move.

61

I looked at his head.

"Guess what? There's something in your hair," I told him.

I looked harder at that thing.

"I think it's a teeny leaf. Or else maybe it's a piece of Kleenex," I said.

He still didn't move.

"Want me to brush it off for you?" I asked. "'Cause that would not be any trouble. And I would be happy to do it."

I waited very patient for him to answer.

Then I tapped on him some more.

"Yeah, only I really think you should do something," I said. "'Cause what if somebody blowed their nose on a teeny Kleenex? And then it flied in the wind. And got stuck in your hair. Did you ever think of that? Huh? 'Cause that would not be pleasant."

He didn't answer.

"Whoever wants me to get the Kleenex out of his hair, raise your hand," I said.

All of a sudden, Handsome Warren uncovered his angry face.

"I thought you weren't going to talk!" he hollered. "I thought you were going to mind your own personal beeswax!"

I smiled very cute.

"Yeah, only I *am* minding my own personal beeswax, Warren," I said. "I just needed to tell you about the teeny Kleenex. And so now I'm all done talking. Period. The end."

Handsome Warren rolled his eyes way up at the sky. He covered up with his arms again.

I waited some more.

"Okay, here's the problem," I said. "The

teeny Kleenex is still there. And so how would you like me to handle this?"

Handsome Warren put his hands over his ears.

"Stop it!" he yelled. "Stop talking to me! Why are you sitting here anyway? Why don't you just go with your stupid friends and leave me alone?"

"'Cause I am being nice, that's why," I said. "Plus also I am understanding your feelings. On account of Mother said that is how I make friends."

Handsome Warren did a grouchy face.

"I'm *not* your friend," he said. "I don't have any friends at this school. All my friends were at my *other* school. But then my dad made me move here. And now nothing is the same. I hate this place! I hate it! I hate it!"

Then he quick hided his head in his knees again. And he started to cry.

He tried to be quiet.

Only I still could hear him sniffling in there.

It made me feel sad inside.

I patted him very gentle.

"Sorry, Warren. Sorry you feel bad. Sorry. Sorry," I said real soft.

Just then a good idea popped in my head.

"Hey. *I* know. Maybe I can get you a Band-Aid. Would you like that, Warren? 'Cause sometimes Band-Aids make things better...

"Or else here's another good idea. Maybe I could tickle you. 'Cause tickling makes you laugh, right? And so I would be glad to give it a try."

I jiggled him.

"Want to try on my golden crown, Warren? Huh? Want to? 'Cause a golden crown makes you feel like a million bucks."

I took it off to give to him.

He didn't take it.

I put my golden crown on the ground.

Then I took off my princess collar and my Cinderella gloves. And I put them on the ground, too.

After that, I sat very still. And I listened to Warren being sad.

Finally I did a sigh. And I tried my very last idea.

"Knock knock," I said.

Handsome Warren didn't answer.

"Knock knock," I said a little bit louder. Then I kept on saying knock knock, until that guy got sick of it.

"OH, ALL RIGHT! WHO'S THERE?" he grouched.

"Hatch," I said.

"Hatch who?" said Handsome Warren.

"HA HA! MADE YOU SNEEZE! GET IT, WARREN? GET IT? YOU SAID *HATCHOO*! DO YOU GET IT?

"Knock knock," I said again.

Handsome Warren peeked one eye at me.

"Who's there?" he said.

"Ash," I said.

"Ash who?" said Handsome Warren.

"HA! I DID IT AGAIN, WARREN! I MADE YOU SNEEZE AGAIN! YOU SAID *ASHOO*! AND SO THAT WAS ANOTHER GOOD ONE, RIGHT?"

Handsome Warren raised up his head. His face didn't look as mad.

"Knock knock," I said.

"Who's there?" said Handsome Warren.

"Kook."

"Kook who?" he said.

I made a fist at that guy.

"Hey! Who are you calling cuckoo, mister?" I said.

Just then, Handsome Warren did a teeny smile.

He waited for a second. Then he smiled some more.

"Knock knock," he said.

"Who's there?"

"Icy," said Handsome Warren.

"Icy who?"

"Icy London, Icy France, Icy Lucille's underpants," he said.

I clapped and clapped.

"Me too, Warren! I saw those things,

too! 'Cause that crazy kook is always twirling around in those bouncy dresses, that's why!"

All of a sudden, my whole face lighted up.

"Knock knock!"

"Who's there?" said Handsome Warren.

"Irish."

"Irish who?"

"IRISH I WAS AN OSCAR MAYER WIENER!" I sang real loud.

Then me and Handsome Warren started laughing real hard! And we holded our sides! And we rolled all around on the ground!

"YOU ARE A NUTBALL!" said Handsome Warren.

"YOU ARE A NUTBALL, TOO!" I said back.

"WE ARE *BOTH* NUTBALLS!" he said.

And so after that, me and Nutball Warren rolled and laughed and rolled and laughed. All around the grass. Till the bell rang!

'Cause that's what nutballs do, of course!

Plus also me and him were brand-new friends, I think!

And that is called *happily ever after*!

Barbara Park says:

"There's nothing cuter than a kindergarten romance. But I have to admit, I was a little bit annoyed with Junie B. when I saw how fast she tried to turn herself into Lucille or Grace, just to interest Handsome Warren!

"Shame on you!" I thought as I wrote. "Just be yourself! He'll like you! I promise!"

Then I had to laugh. Because it's the *exact* same advice my mother gave me (at least a kajillion times).

Okay, Mom...I *get* it now...

And (I'm hoping) so does Junie B.**"**